MW01110151

lapa
PUBLISHERS

Original title: *Z is vir Zackie: Die rowwe resies*

© Publication: LAPA Publishers (Pty) Ltd
380 Bosman Street, Pretoria
Tel. 012 401 0700
E-mail: lapa@lapa.co.za
© Text: Jaco Jacobs 2016
© Illustrations: Alex van Houwelingen 2016
English translation by Melinda van der Molen

Set in 16 pt on 25 pt Garamond Book Education
Cover design by Zinelda McDonald
Set by Full Circle
Printed by Novus Print, a division of Novus Holdings

First English edition 2020

ISBN 978 0 7993 9755 0

Jaco Jacobs
Z IS FOR ZACK

Illustrations
Alex
van
Houwelingen

READY TO RACE

LAPA Publishers
www.lapa.co.za

This is Zack.

He lives in a yellow house.

The house is in Zucchini Street.

Today, Zack and Vincent are in the garden.

On the lawn are tins of paint.

Zack and Vincent are working hard.

A lady peeps over the wall.

It is Mrs Longbottom.

She is always grumpy.

'What are you two doing?' she asks.

'I hope you are not making mischief again.'

'We are painting our go-kart,' says
Zack. 'My dad built it.'

'There is a race at school tomorrow,'
says Vincent. 'We are going to take
part.'

'Oh,' mutters Mrs Longbottom. 'Well,
it looks like a good go-kart. I also had
a go-kart when I was younger.'

Vincent and Zack look at each other.

Mrs Longbottom in a go-kart?

That must look very funny!

'Good luck with the race,' says Mrs Longbottom.

She sounds less grumpy.

Zack and Vincent start painting again.

Soon, they are done.

'It looks very good,' says Vincent.

'It looks very fast,' says Zack.

'It looks very silly,' says a voice.

It is Brett.

Brett is a bully.

He likes hurting other children.

He does not like to lose.

'Are you taking part in the Big Go-kart Race?' asks Brett.

Zack and Vincent nod.

Brett laughs.

'I am going to win! My go-kart is very fast. My dad bought it for me. It was very expensive. Your go-kart looks like a baby's pram.'

Zack does not like being teased.
'This is a good go-kart,' he says.
'Mrs Longbottom also says so.'
Brett snorts. 'What does an old lady
know about go-karts?' he says.

The next day is Friday.

Zack and Vincent arrive at school early.

Zack's dad has brought the go-kart.

'You have done a good paint job,' he

says. 'I hope you boys win. Good luck!'

Zack smiles proudly.

13

Here comes Brett.

His dad has also brought his go-kart.

It is much bigger than Zack's.

It looks much fancier than Zack's.

It looks much faster than Zack's.

Zack's sister, Kate, wants to take a
photo.
'Smile,' she says.
Zack pulls a funny face.
He does not like it when Kate takes
photos.

'Good morning, everyone,' says the headmaster. 'Welcome to the Big Go-kart Race.'

There are lots of go-karts.

There are lots of people.

They have all come to the see the race.

'Wow, Zack,' says a boy. 'Your go-kart is great.'

'My go-kart is better,' brags Brett. 'It was very expensive.'

'We will see whose go-kart is the fastest,' says a voice.

Zack turns round.

It is Mrs Longbottom.

She has also come to see the race.

It is still a while before the race begins.
Zack and Vincent walk around.
They look at all the fancy go-karts.
Zack's sister takes more photos.

'Get ready, everyone,' says the headmaster.

The race is about to start.

Zack is very excited.

He gets into the go-kart.

Vincent pushes him to the starting line.

Brett also sits in his go-kart.

A big boy will push his go-kart.

The boy looks strong.

The boy looks fast.

Brett looks at Zack and Vincent.

He sticks out his tongue.

Zack grits his teeth.

'Are you ready, Vincent?' he whispers.

They have to win today!

The headmaster starts the countdown.
'Three … two … one … go!'
The start gun fires.
They are on their way.
'Go, Zack and Vincent! Go!' shouts
Mrs Longbottom.

Zack and Vincent are as quick as
lightning.
Their kart is very fast.
Brett is ahead.
Zack and Vincent catch up with him.
Zack is smiling.

Suddenly there is a loud bang.

Thwack!

Their kart races off the track.

There is dust everywhere.

Zack falls very hard.

Brett looks over his shoulder. He laughs.

Zack gets up. He dusts himself off.
'What happened?' he groans.
Vincent sighs. 'The wheel has fallen
off our go-kart.'
Oh no!
They are going to lose the race.

Here comes Mrs Longbottom.
'Fasten the wheel,' she calls.
Zack shakes his head. 'We do not
have a screwdriver,' he says.
Mrs Longbottom opens her handbag.
'Here,' she says. 'Use this.'
She gives Zack a nail file.

Zack takes the nail file.

He tries to fasten the wheel.

It works!

'Thank you, Mrs Longbottom!' he says.

Zack gets back into the go-kart.

'Push, Vincent!' he calls out.

They are now last in the race.

Zack and Vincent race like the wind.

One by one they pass the other children.

They are nearly at the finish line.

There is still one go-kart ahead of them.

'I am going to win!' shouts Brett. He laughs.

Vincent runs faster.

But it is too late.

Brett is first to cross the finish line.

Zack and Vincent come second.

The headmaster stands up and says,

'The winner of the Big Go-kart Race is ...'

'Wait!' says a voice.

Kate comes running.

She shows her camera to the headmaster.

'Just look at this photo,' she says.

The headmaster frowns. He looks at the photo. His face turns red.

'Brett!' he says. 'Did you loosen the wheel on Zack and Vincent's go-kart?'

'No, sir!' says Brett.

The headmaster holds up the camera.
Everyone looks at the photo.
On the photo it is clear that Brett is
loosening the wheel.
'Brett cheated,' says the headmaster.
'The winners of the Big Go-kart Race
are … Zack and Vincent!'
Everyone cheers.
Zack and Vincent are happy.
They have won the Big Go-kart Race!

That afternoon they walk over to
Mrs Longbottom's house.
They knock on the door.
She opens the door.
'Thank you very much for the nail
file, Mrs Longbottom,' says Zack.
'It was a clever plan.'
Mrs Longbottom smiles.
'The two of you deserved to
win,' she says. 'May I ask
you a favour? It's been years
since I had a ride in
a go-kart …'

A while
later a go-
kart races down
Zucchini Street.
The go-kart is red and
yellow.
Zack and Vincent are behind the
go-kart. They push as fast as they can.
Mrs Longbottom is riding in the go-kart.
She shrieks with joy.
Wheeeeee!